# Careers
## Las Carreras

by Mary Berendes • illustrated by Kathleen Petelinsek

**A note from the Publisher:**
In general, nouns and descriptive words in Spanish end in "o" when referring to males, and in "a" when referring to females. The words in this book reflect their corresponding illustrations.

## The Child's World®

Published in the United States of America by The Child's World®
1980 Lookout Drive • Mankato, MN 56003-1705
800-599-READ • www.childsworld.com

**Acknowledgments**
The Child's World®: Mary Berendes, Publishing Director
The Design Lab: Kathleen Petelinsek, Design and Page Production

Language Adviser: Ariel Strichartz

**Library of Congress Cataloging-in-Publication Data**
Berendes, Mary.
 Careers = Las carreras / by Mary Berendes ;
illustrated by Kathleen Petelinsek.
   p. cm. — (Wordbooks = Libros de palabras)
 ISBN 978-1-59296-988-3 (library bound : alk. paper)
 1. Occupations—Terminology—Juvenile literature.
I. Petelinsek, Kathleen.
II. Title. III. Title: Carreras. IV. Series.
 HB2581.B436 2008
 331.7003—dc22                    2007046563

**clerk**
el dependiente

**bag**
la bolsa

**groceries**
los comestibles

**apron**
el delantal

**grocer**
el tendero

3

**dentist**
la dentista

**mouth**
la boca

**teeth**
los dientes

**mask**
la mascarilla

**toothbrush**
el cepillo
de dientes

4

**nurse**
la enfermera

**chart**
el historial
médico

**doctor**
el médico

**stethoscope**
el estetoscopio

**scrubs**
el uniforme de
personal médico

**helmet**
el casco

**police officer**
el agente de
policía

**ax**
el hacha

**badge**
la placa

**firefighter**
la bombera

6

7

**chef**
la chef

**spatula**
la paleta

**pan**
la sartén

**waiter**
el camarero

**baker**
la panadera

**oven mitts**
los guantes
para el horno

**cookies**
las galletas

9

**coach**
la entrenadora

**teacher**
el maestro

**books**
los libros

**basketball**
el baloncesto

**principal**
el director

**librarian**
la bibliotecaria

**glasses**
las gafas

**suit**
el traje

11

**school bus**
el autobús
escolar

SCHOOL BUS

**bus driver**
el conductor

**tire**
el neumático

**road**
la calle

**outside mirror**
el espejo lateral

**truck**
el camión

**truck driver**
la camionera

**bumper**
el parachoques

**mechanic**
el mecánico

**flashlight**
la linterna

**wrench**
la llave
inglesa

**coveralls**
el mono

14

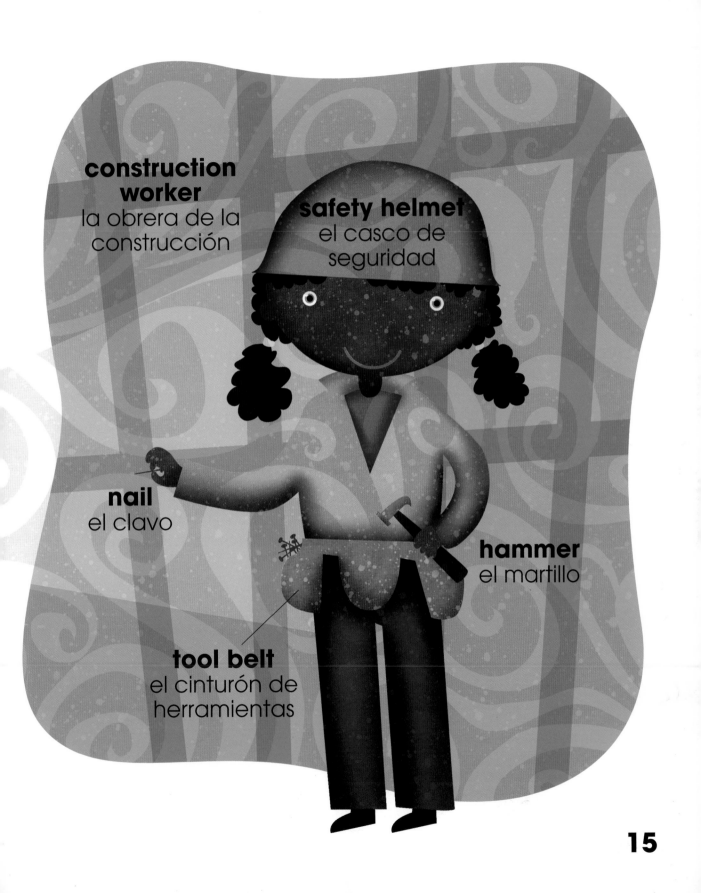

**construction worker**
la obrera de la construcción

**safety helmet**
el casco de seguridad

**nail**
el clavo

**hammer**
el martillo

**tool belt**
el cinturón de herramientas

15

**scientist**
la científica

**goggles**
las gafas
protectoras

**test tubes**
las probetas

**experiment**
el experimento

**lab coat**
la bata de
laboratorio

**Earth**
la Tierra

**stars**
las estrellas

**space suit**
el traje
espacial

**astronaut**
el astronauta

17

**cloud**
la nube

**pilot**
la pilota

**tie**
la corbata

**suitcase**
la maleta

18

**letter carrier**
la cartera

**mail**
el correo

19

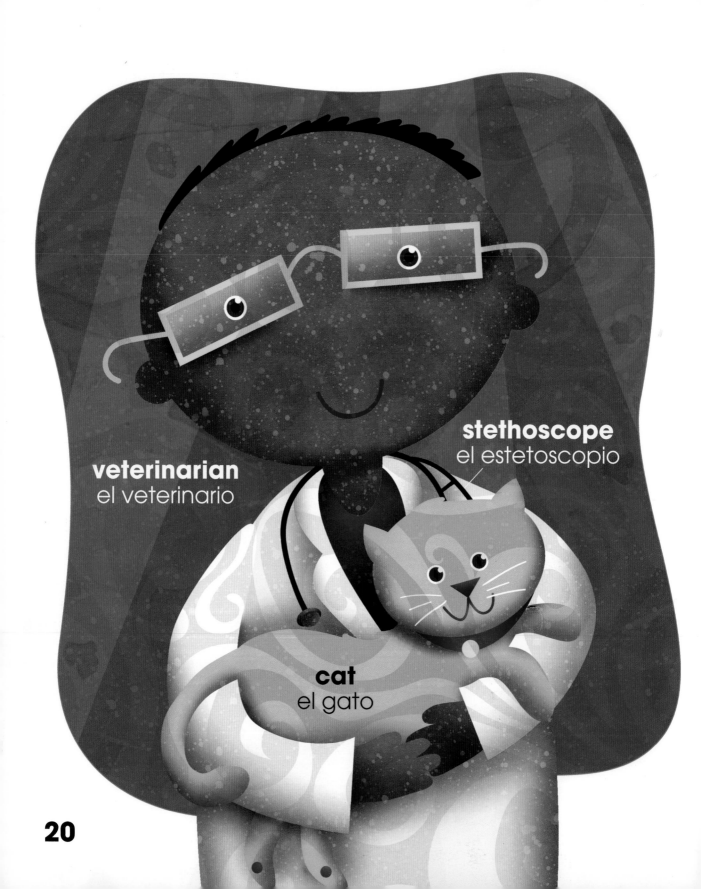

**veterinarian**
el veterinario

**stethoscope**
el estetoscopio

**cat**
el gato

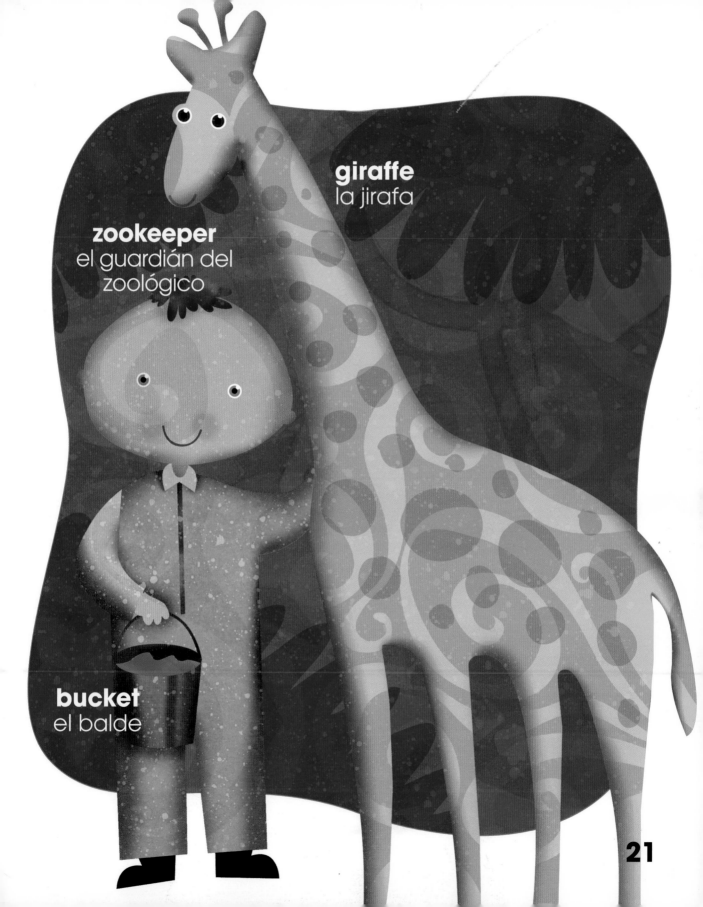

**giraffe**
la jirafa

**zookeeper**
el guardián del
zoológico

**bucket**
el balde

**megaphone**
el megáfono

**lifeguard**
la socorrista

22

**artist**
la artista

**canvas**
el lienzo

**paintbrush**
el pincel

**easel**
el caballete

**paint**
la pintura

23

# word list
## lista de palabras

| | | | |
|---|---|---|---|
| **apron** | el delantal | **lifeguard** | la socorrista |
| **artist** | la artista | **mail** | el correo |
| **astronaut** | el astronauta | **mask** | la mascarilla |
| **ax** | el hacha | **mechanic** | el mecánico |
| **badge** | la placa | **megaphone** | el megafono |
| **bag (paper)** | la bolsa | **nail** | el clavo |
| **baker** | la panadera | **notes** | las notas |
| **basketball** | el baloncesto | **nurse** | la enfermera |
| **books** | los libros | **outside mirror** | el espejo lateral |
| **bucket** | el balde | **oven mitts** | los guantes para el horno |
| **bumper** | el parachoques | **paint** | la pintura |
| **bus driver** | el conductor | **paintbrush** | el pincel |
| **camera** | la cámera | **pan** | la sartén |
| **canvas** | el lienzo | **photographer** | la fotógrafa |
| **cat** | el gato | **pilot** | la pilota |
| **chart (medical)** | el historial médico | **police officer** | el agente de policía |
| **chef** | la chef | **principal** | el director |
| **clerk** | el dependiente | **reporter** | el periodista |
| **cloud** | la nube | **road** | la calle |
| **coach** | la entrenadora | **safety helmet** | el casco de seguridad |
| **construction worker** | la obrera de la construcción | **school bus** | el autobus escolar |
| | | **scientist** | la científica |
| **cookies** | las galletas | **scrubs** | el uniforme de personal médico |
| **coveralls** | el mono | **space suit** | el traje espacial |
| **dentist** | la dentista | **spatula** | la paleta |
| **doctor** | el médico | **stars** | las estrellas |
| **Earth** | la Tierra | **stethoscope** | el estetoscopio |
| **easel** | el caballete | **suit** | el traje |
| **experiment** | el experimento | **suitcase** | la maleta |
| **firefighter** | la bombera | **teacher** | el maestro |
| **flashlight** | la linterna | **test tubes** | las probetas |
| **giraffe** | la jirafa | **tie** | la corbata |
| **glasses** | las gafas | **tire** | el neumático |
| **goggles** | las gafas protectoras | **tool belt** | el cinturón de herramientas |
| **grocer** | el tendero | **truck** | el camión |
| **groceries** | los comestibles | **truck driver** | la camionera |
| **hammer** | el martillo | **veterinarian** | el veterinario |
| **helmet** | el casco | **waiter** | el camarero |
| **lab coat** | la bata de laboratorio | **wrench** | la llave inglesa |
| **letter carrier** | la cartera | **zookeeper** | el guardian del zoológico |
| **librarian** | la bibliotecaria | | |